THIS BOOK IS THE PROPERTY OF

. . . .

DUST 'N' BONES
by Chris Mould

First published in 2006
by Hodder Children's Books

Text and illustrations copyright © Chris Mould 2006

Hodder Children's Books
338 Euston Road, London NW1 3BH

Hodder Children's Books Australia
Level 17/207 Kent Street, Sydney, NSW 2000

The right of Chris Mould to be identified as the author and the
illustrator of this Work has been asserted by him in accordance
with the Copyright, Designs and Patents Act 1988.

A catalogue record of this book
is available from the British Library.

ISBN: 978 0 340 89327 2
10 9 8 7 6 5 4 3 2 1

Colour reproduction by Dot Gradations. Ltd. UK
Printed in China

Hodder Children's Books is a division of
Hachette Children's Books, an Hachette Livre UK Company

Dust 'n' Bones

Ten terrifying classic and
original ghost stories,
adapted, written and illustrated by

Chris Mould

Hodder
Children's
Books

A division of Hachette Children's Books

Hello Stranger,
did you lose your way?

Don't you know it's not safe

to travel at night in these parts?

Something or somebody's going to pick up your trail

before long. You never know what you might meet

around here at this hour.

You're miles from anywhere and there's a storm

coming in. Perhaps I should put you on the right road.

I don't mind. It'll give me some company.

Maybe I'll tell you some tales along the way.

Contents

The Legend of Sleepy Hollow

By Washington Irving

Adapted by Chris Mould

When the Hallowe'en party had slowed down the fireside talk turned to ghosts.

'Did you ever hear of the Headless Horseman of Sleepy Hollow?' asked Brom Bones. Ichabod Crane nodded his head and said that yes, possibly, he had.

Brom Bones liked nothing more than to tell a good ghost story and Sleepy Hollow abounded with such tales, for it held a drowsy, dreamy influence over its people and they would often talk of nightmares and strange visions. If there was one particular vision that gripped the people of Sleepy Hollow firmly it was the sight of this headless figure on horseback, hurrying along in the gloom of night as if on the wings of the wind, searching for his lost head high and low. Mostly he is seen on the dark road to the church where he transforms into a skeleton before disappearing in a clap of thunder.

Brom Bones loved to tell his own story and brag about the time
he had offered to race the ghostly rider for a bowl of punch and that
he would have beaten him but when they reached the church bridge
the headless spectre had vanished in a *flash of fire*.

Ichabod laughed nervously at the tale. He had enjoyed
the storytelling but knew that it was past midnight and
he must now face the lonesome highway alone.

Ichabod was the new schoolmaster. A tall gangly figure with feet like barges, narrow shoulders and a body that hung awkwardly out of his clothes. With huge ears and a long snipe of a nose, he was a sight to be seen, for sure. He, too, liked a good ghost story. Yes, there were times when he even frightened himself with his own tales. He was a popular character and admired for his stories, not to mention his wonderful singing voice. And oh, what a dancer he was. Ichabod Crane was no ordinary schoolmaster.

Now both he and Brom Bones had their eyes fixed on the same girl. Young Katerina Van Tassel. And whenever Brom saw the lanky schoolmaster smile upon Katerina a jealousy stirred inside him.

On this particular night Brom hadn't managed one dance with Katerina. Instead he had watched Ichabod whisk her off her feet and sing to her like a lark and he swore to himself that he would have his revenge. It was when they sat around the fire telling tales that Brom was determined to outdo Ichabod with his stories.

Ichabod stepped out into the night. He would have preferred to have stayed around the fire and a shiver ran through him as he climbed up on to Gunpowder, his trusty horse. He turned and headed for home.

As he made his way along the dusty road out of town he began to sing along to himself but his voice trembled nervously. Shortly, he felt that something or someone was upon him. He should have been relieved to find himself in company – but not this time. Through the mist he could just make out the shape of a huge, black horse and its rider. It seemed to be following, matching his pace. Ichabod had no relish for this strange midnight companion and urged Gunpowder to walk faster.

The stranger quickened his horse, also, and stayed on his shoulder. Ichabod pulled up and fell into a walk, hoping to lag behind. The other did the same. Ichabod's heart sank. He turned to grasp a glimpse of his midnight companion and was horror-struck to find that not only was he headless – but that he carried his head before him as he rode...

His terror rose to desperation: he rained a shower of kicks and blows upon Gunpowder, hoping to give his companion the slip, but the spectre stayed on him.

Away they dashed through thick and thin, stones flying and sparks flashing at every bound. Ichabod's flimsy garments fluttered in the air, as he stretched his long, lank body over his horse's head in the eagerness of his flight.

They had now reached the point where the road forks. Instead of steering off to the right and the comfort of the school house, Gunpowder,

who *seemed possessed by a demon*, took the opposite turn and plunged

headlong downhill. This road lead through a sandy hollow,

shaded by trees, and ended where the bridge opens the way to

a grassy knoll. Here was where the church stood.

Just as Ichabod got halfway through the hollow, the girths of the

saddle gave way and he felt it slip from under him. He could only save

himself by grasping the horse's neck. Ichabod held on for dear life.

Hearing the saddle being trampled underfoot, and remembering Brom's

story, he knew that he need only hang on until he reached the church bridge before his companion disappeared.

Just then he felt the horseman grow even closer. He fancied he could feel the horse's hot breath down the nape of his neck. As Gunpowder cantered over the bridge Ichabod risked a glimpse behind him to see if his companion would truly disappear. As he did so, the ghostly horseman took his severed head and *hurled it towards him.*

Ichabod took the full force of the missile and tumbled headlong into the dust.

The next day, old Gunpowder was found quietly cropping the grass near to the bridge. At his feet lay Ichabod's hat and the remains of a shattered pumpkin.

Poor old Ichabod was never to be seen again.

Shortly after, Katerina Van Tassel married Brom Bones and some say that he had more to do with the outcome of this story than he reckons.

Others think they know better.

Except perhaps for Brom Bones.

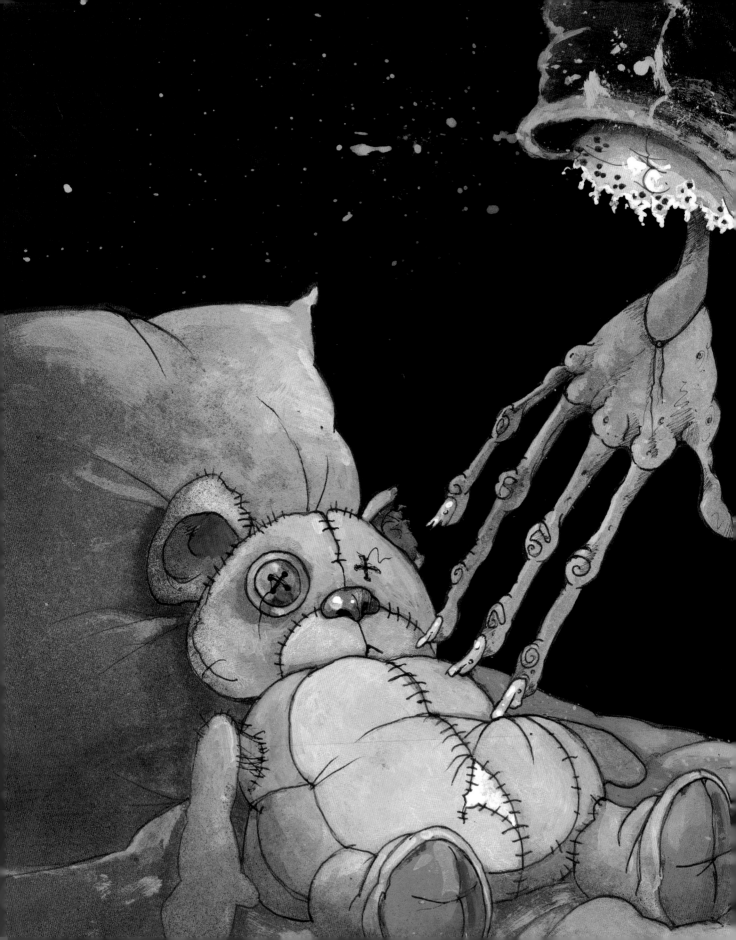

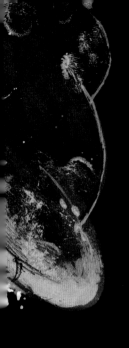

A·Bedtime Tale·

By Chris Mould

Did you ever wake in the night – too afraid to open your eyes? *Yes?*

Then you were right not to! And there's a good reason for it.

Did you ever think that you could feel the weight of something pressing down on the end of your bed, like someone was sitting there? And you thought that they were staring right at you but you just *couldn't look! Did you?*

Well you were right about that too. There was someone there. They were staring.

Perhaps you thought you could smell a stink of outside, all musty and damp, of soil and gravestones and freezing cold rain!

Oh, that was him all right.

Mister Midnight.

That's what they call him.

And you'd better be careful because if ever you do open those tired little eyes he will swallow you up in one gulp.

But keep them shut and he can't touch you!

Hold on to them tight and don't let go. Because if they spring open – even for just one second – that's it. You're gone.

You will hear his heart galloping around his ribcage with hungry excitement. And you might even hear his starving stomach rolling and rumbling like thunder, but whatever you do, keep your eyes pressed tight and don't open them until morning or he'll make a quick meal out of you and that's for sure.

How do I know?

How do I know that he creeps in from the night like a spectral intruder through gaps in the floors and walls with *scratchety long-fingered hands?*

How do I know that he sits there cross-legged with *staring fiery eyes* and an aching empty belly, with a dying candle that flickers at you and teases your lids open?

How do I know that he's dressed in *black with muddy boots and an ugly wide-brimmed hat* and a face that matches, with a beak of a nose and a shock of white hair trailing on his filthy coat?

How do I know?

Well, that's simple. Because it's me, of course. How else would I know?

And I'll tell you something more, my friend.
Tonight I'll be sitting on your bed...

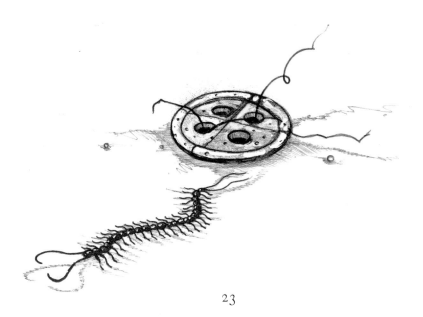

23

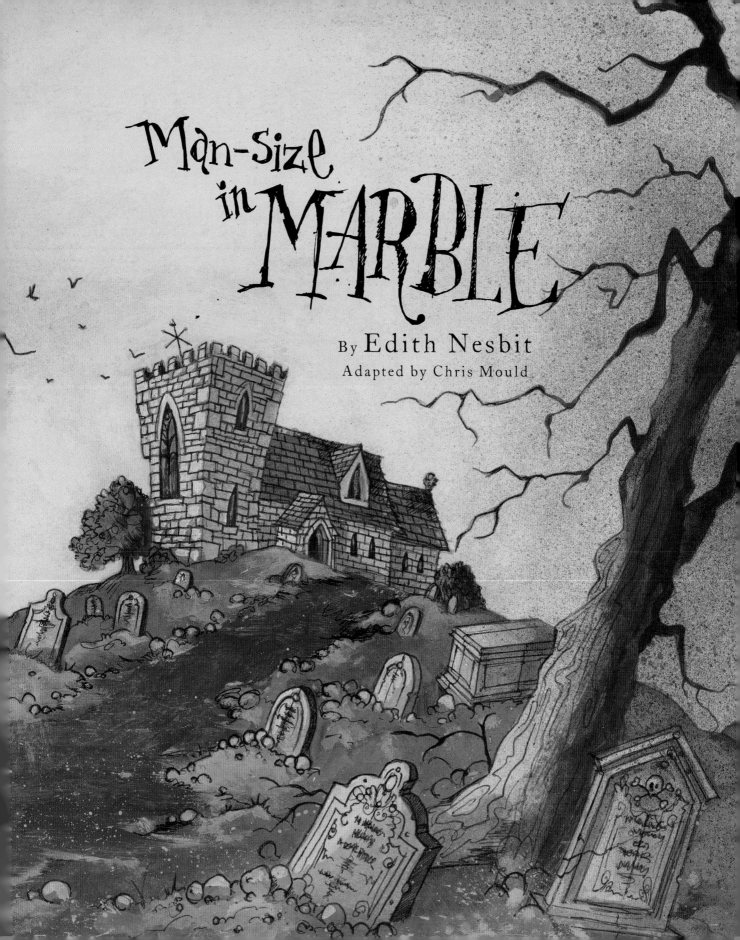

Man-size in MARBLE

By Edith Nesbit

Adapted by Chris Mould

There were two of them. Identical and placed on either side of the altar in the village church, each was a grey marble figure of a knight in full battle armour. With shield and sword at their side they held their hands upward in everlasting prayer.

Their names were long forgotten but local people told of their reputations as fierce and evil villains, guilty of deeds so foul that the house in which they lived, which had stood on the site of our cottage, had been struck by lightning as an act of vengeance from heaven. And despite all this, the riches of their heirs had bought them a place in the church. I had looked at the cold hard faces of marble and believed that what I heard could well be true.

'I should be glad to leave before the end of the month sir,' requested Mrs Dorman, our housekeeper.

'Is there a problem?' I had asked. She had only been with us for the short time since we had bought the house, about three months altogether.

'None at all sir. You have both been most kind,' came her answer. I pressed her further and eventually she sank into her admission. 'Well sir,' she began, 'you may have seen, in the church beside the altar, two bodies drawn out man-size in marble.'

I told her that since Laura and I had bought the cottage we often walked up to the church and that we were both familiar with what she described.

She continued: '*Well, they do say that on Hallowe'en them two bodies gets up from their slabs and walks down the aisle in their marble. And as the clock strikes eleven they walks out of the church door and over the graves and if it's a wet night there's the marks of their feet in the morning.*'

'And where do they go?' I asked in fascination.

'*They comes back here to their old home sir, and if anyone meets them...*'

But not another word could I get from her except
a stern warning to lock the door early on Hallowe'en.
I did not tell Laura of the marble shapes that
walked in the night. A legend concerning our
house might trouble her. Maybe I would
mention it when the time had passed.
Soon I ceased to think of the story at all.
I never had much faith in the supernatural.
Mrs Dorman was due to leave on
the Thursday. That day came and went.
The Friday passed in the usual way:
with Mrs Dorman absent Laura
and I shared the housework in
the morning and relaxed
in the afternoon.

But something was bothering Laura.

'I'm rather uneasy,' she admitted. 'I am shivering a great deal and I feel that something evil is upon us.' I reassured her and we sat quietly for a while, taking in the fire.

At about half-past ten I decided I would take a late evening walk. I suggested Laura should get some sleep and I left her in peace.

What a night it was. Dark clouds rolled around and it was deathly silent. The church tower stood out against the sky. The bell sounded. Eleven already? I would just take a moment inside before wandering back.

Treading the pathway to the church I was sure I heard footsteps. Echoes of my own perhaps. Then I noticed the church door was open. Suddenly I remembered the legend of the marble figures. This was the very moment they were supposed to rise up and walk from their slabs. I could do no less than walk up to the altar, and then I could assure myself that the legend was nonsense and inform Mrs Dorman that the figures had slept soundly in the ghostly hour.

I stopped short. My heart gave a great leap that nearly choked me and then it sank sickeningly. The figures were gone and the marble slabs lay bare in the moonlight that shone through the west window.

Were they really gone or was I mad? I passed my hand over the smooth slabs and felt their flat unbroken surface. They really were gone.

A horror seized me. I tore down the aisle and out of the church.

Outside I met a figure in the darkness. It was Doctor Kelly, our neighbour, on his way home from visiting a patient.

'The marble figures have gone from the church!' I gasped. I was trembling as I spoke.

He broke into a laugh and in a few moments he had calmed me and suggested we go back and take another look. We headed inside and walked up the aisle.

Doctor Kelly struck a match. *'Here they are,'* he said. *'Ye've been dreaming or drinking if you don't mind me saying.'*

I opened my eyes. The two shapes lay there.

'It must have been a trick of the light,' I said.

He was busy leaning over and looking at the right hand. He struck another match. *'This hand is broken,'* he pointed out.

And so it was. I was sure it had been intact the last time Laura and I had been there. But now was not the time for thought. *'Come along,'* I said, *'or my wife will be getting anxious.'* I invited him back for a drink and he accepted. As we walked up the path, bright light streamed out of the open door. I was sure I had shut it behind me. Had Laura gone out?

At first we did not see her. The window was open and the draught had set all the candles flaring one way. I turned to the window and there she was, in the recess. A look of fear on her face.

She had fallen back against a table, and her body lay half on it and half on the window seat with her head hanging down. Her eyes were wide open but now they saw nothing. What had they last seen to terrify her face into such an expression of horror?

I ran to her and cradled her in my arms. Her hands were tightly clenched. In one of them she held something fast. When I was quite sure she was dead I let the doctor open it so that we might see what she held.

It was a grey marble finger.

The Stranger

By Chris Mould

R alph was bouncing down the road wearing his widest grin. The truck bumped and thudded at every turn. It was late and there was nobody else in sight. He put his foot down on the accelerator and steered his way through another blind corner.

Screeeeeeeeeeech.

A full moon glared down on the road and lit the way, aiding his broken headlamp.

Up ahead someone, or something, stood at the side of the road. Ralph slowed down. It looked like the figure of a man and he was holding out his hand as if to stop him.

The truck came to a halt and skidded slightly on the dusty tarmac surface. A pile of boxes and cartons toppled over and spread across the open back of the vehicle where the dog lay sleeping. He jumped up and barked. 'Get down Duke.'

Ralph opened the door and stared at the hitcher. He was tall and thin and dressed in black. He held some luggage in his hand. His eyes were slant and shifty. There was a few days' growth in his beard and he looked as if he had been walking for some time.

'I wouldn't hang around here too long if I were you,' said Ralph, hanging out of the doorway, 'You never know who you might come across!'

'Just need to get to town,' he answered. 'Can I jump in?'

Ralph hesitated before he replied. He looked him up and down again.

'Sure,' he said. 'As long as you don't mind a bumpy ride?'

'It's not a problem,' the hitcher insisted, and he pulled himself up into the seat. He was a stern looking man and though he hadn't managed to turn up the corners of his mouth and smile, he still thanked him for stopping.

With a spin of his back wheel Ralph was off again. Shortly, he was back up to full speed. Tearing along like a wild dog through the dusty landscape. He took a sideways glance at his companion. He didn't look too good. Come to think of it, he didn't smell too good. Maybe it was the night air.

He didn't say too much either. He seemed the shy, quiet sort. Ralph was used to the odd hitcher now and again. He wasn't the sort to be put off. He knew a sinister character when he saw one, he thought to himself. Perhaps it was the nagging doubt that something was wrong that made him go that little bit faster, knowing that the sooner he got to town the sooner he would be rid of this silent stranger.

He rattled along. *Crash, thump, thump.* The dog jumped up again. A sharp bark came from the back. 'Quiet Duke,' Ralph called.

The hitcher stared into the darkness ahead. Never moving or saying

a word. His sharp eyes were fixed on the winding road as they climbed the hill to the top. His black shape remained unshaken as he held tight onto his seat.

'Nearly there,' said Ralph as they bounded into another corner. The truck squeaked and groaned with every move. Whoever this midnight traveller was he was sure getting the ride of his life.

Eventually they were up on the tops and they could see the twinkle of the lights down in the town. They drew closer. 'You can leave me at the truck stop,' suggested the hitcher, as they passed the illuminated windows of the truck café.

Screeech. Ralph pulled up.

The man climbed out and Ralph was on his way in a cloud of dust, happy to be alone again with his dog springing up and down in the back like a jack in a box.

The traveller stepped into the café.

'Are you all right sir?' came a voice. A girl stood at the counter.

'Just had a bit of a bumpy ride, that's all. Some crazy truck driver and his dog frightened me half to death. He was driving like a maniac. Nearly killed me. I broke down earlier this afternoon and had to leave my car in a ditch. Had to hitch my way here!'

'Was it a pick-up? A rusty old heap in yellow with a missing headlamp? Crazy little guy with a mad dog?'

'Yes, yes, that was him.'

The girl stepped closer to him. 'You've just taken a ghost ride with crazy old Ralph. It was his driving that killed him in the first place. Him and his darned dog. Couldn't keep his foot off the accelerator. Next time you'd better be more choosy who you take a ride with. You're lucky to be alive...'

The Tell-Tale Heart

By Edgar Allan Poe

Adapted by Chris Mould

Mad? Why would you think me mad?

I can't say how the idea entered my head, but once it had it haunted me night and day. I had great affection for the old man and he never caused me to dislike him. He had not insulted me and I had no desire for his belongings.

I think it was his eye! Yes, it was. One of his eyes appeared to me like the eye of a vulture. It was pale and blue and whenever it gazed upon me my blood ran cold. Eventually I made up my mind to be rid of the old man and be free of this eye for ever.

Now I know you still think me mad, but listen. You should have seen how carefully I went about my plan. I was never kinder to the old man than during the week before I killed him.

Every night at midnight I made up my mind to do the deed. I turned the latch of his door and, oh so gently, I peered inside. I concealed a lantern at my side. Oh, you would have laughed to see how cunningly I placed my head through the door. Slowly, slowly, so as not to disturb the old man's slumber. It took me a whole hour to get my head through the door so I could see him laid upon his bed.

Now tell me, what madman would be so careful as this?

And then I held up the lantern so that a single beam of light touched upon the eye. But while the eye was shut the task was unnecessary. For seven long hours through every night I watched, and in the morning I would speak heartily to him and would ask how he had slept.

But on the eighth night I fumbled at the latch and caused the old man to sit up and cry out. 'Who's there?'

I kept still and silent. When I had waited a long time I peered through the tiniest crevice to see that the eye was wide open and I grew furious as I gazed upon it. It glared out of the darkness like a torchlight. The rest of him faded out into the blackness of his room.

Then I heard a low dull sound. A sound I knew well. It was the beating of the man's heart and it increased my anger. It grew quicker and louder. So loud I thought it might burst. A new anxiety seized me.

What if a neighbour should hear it?

I burst into the room and dragged him to the floor. He shrieked once – and once only. I pulled the bed over him and in an instant the old man was stone dead. His eye would trouble me no more.

Perhaps you still think me mad. You won't, when you hear how cautious I was in concealing the body beneath the floor. Oh, I was so quiet in removing the boards. Not a mark did I make upon the wooden grain and not a single nail did I bend in the process.

By this time it was four in the morning and a knocking came at the door. Three men. Officers of the police. A shriek was heard by a neighbour in the night, they said, and foul deeds were suspected.

The shriek, I said, was my own, in a dream or nightmare. I let them search the house. What had I to fear? The old man was away, I said.

In the enthusiasm of my confidence I brought chairs into that room. I placed my own over the very spot. The officers were satisfied and we were at ease. They chatted for some time.

But then I felt myself grow pale and wished them gone. My head ached and I felt a ringing in my ears, but still they sat and talked. The ringing turned to a low dull noise and I realised it was not in my ears. It was the noise I knew so well. The thumping heartbeat. The officers did not hear it. I spoke loudly to disguise it.

It grew louder still. What could I do?

I paced the floor heavily. I dragged my chair across the boards. I swung it above my head. I ranted and raved. I shouted. Still they chatted pleasantly.

They heard it. They knew. They were mocking me. I was sure of it. I could bear it no longer.

'I ADMIT IT!' I cried.

'Tear up the planks, here, here,' I screamed, pointing at the floor.

'Here is where the beating of that hideous heart lies.'

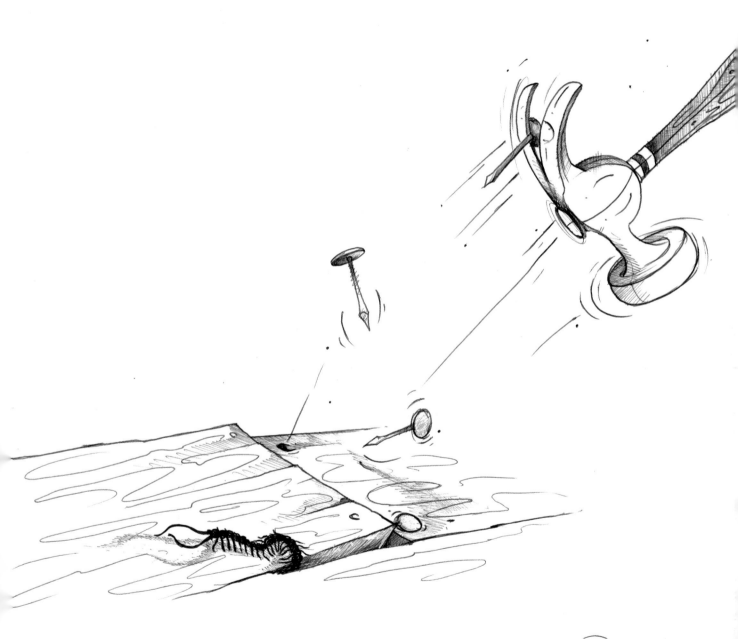

By the Fireside

By Chris Mould

The fire had been glowing all night. The flames had settled down but the coals still burned intensely, all pumpkin orange and toffee-apple red. The snow was falling outside. It rested on the window ledge and was reaching up the pane, obscuring the view. The only sound was the cracking and sparking of the fuel. The twins sat on the rug. They held their cups in their hands and stared into the dancing flames.

'Actually, I do have a ghost story,' announced Mister Ashby from his chair, 'and I can tell you every detail, for it was something that happened to my grandfather as a young man and he wrote it all down when he was older.'

He went to the cupboard and pulled out some papers. 'Here it is,' he said. And he began to read:

'I was orphaned as a young boy and sent to live with my auntie and uncle, who had never had any children of their own. Their house was a huge place. It had stood for over three hundred years and I was haunted by thoughts of the secrets it might contain. Was there something in its past that threw a dark shadow over the house? Or was it my own anxieties that made me feel ill at ease?

My room was on the far right-hand side of the building and overlooked the driveway. A fireplace was centred on the far wall, part of the gable end, and an old mirror hung over the mantelpiece. The room itself had not been used in some time. The air was filled with a damp, musty smell and it was icy cold. A neat pile of logs was

stacked up on one side in the hearth and I obtained permission to light
the fire – both to provide heat and dry out the damp.

The fire seemed to make no difference though I kept it burning as
often as I could. I did like the old place, yet something troubled me and
I was unable to decipher exactly what it was.

One morning I found something whilst making my bed.
On the floor, wedged between two boards was a tooth. Not human,
it was too small. Likely it was from a cat or something similar.
I felt perhaps it would bring me luck and I kept it under my pillow.

But at night I tossed and turned. Something disturbed me in my
sleep, as if to try and waken me. When I did awaken, I felt so frightened
that my heart thumped inside my chest until it hurt. In the end, I think
I must have dropped off to sleep again, for I remember a strange dream.

In the dream I could see my room from the bed and although it was
in darkness the shape of something small could be seen leaping and
crawling around the walls. What it was, I couldn't tell you. Two legged
or four, I wasn't sure. A scratching sound grated in my ears. And then
a face, a ghastly staring face with sharp teeth looking close into my eyes
with its head tilted to one side.

I awoke with a jump. I looked around me. I could see nothing. But the scratching... still, it was there, from the wall where the fireplace stood. Not just scratching but scurrying. And unless I imagined it, a squeal or cackle. Faint, but high pitched. It seemed to last all night and my fear was so great I could not rest but, at length, I grew so tired that I must have gone back to sleep and was in my bed until almost lunchtime.

After that I could not feel comfortable for I feared the house held a dark secret of some kind. In the daylight I was happy, but darkness seemed to pull a sinister cloak around my room and the uneasy feeling I had had in the beginning would not let go of me.

Soon I lived in fear of the night and its visitors. The small tooth I thought would bring me luck seemed only to do me harm. I removed it from under my pillow but I was wary of discarding it, for I felt that to do so might bring me more trouble.

In the end I managed to persuade my aunt to give me another room through some weak excuse I had made. I was then able to live and sleep in peace but still I held a fear about the place.

Many years later I left the house and attended university in the north. After this I left England to work in Italy. I kept in good contact with my auntie and uncle although my visits were sparse and when they passed away I inherited the old place.

On my return to the house, I decided to sell up and buy a property in Italy and I spent the next few months dealing with the sale. Whilst clearing out some papers I came across some old parchment rolled up and filed in a box in the cellar. It related the story of a legend concerning the house and was dated 1760. It read as follows:

"There was, at one time, a small boy living here. Unbeknown to his family he kept a small tame monkey as a pet, keeping it hidden inside the back of the hearth in his room and bringing it out whenever he could. At night he would feed it scraps from the kitchens and let it out through the window on to the roof tiles. To keep it hidden he had fashioned a false panel inside the fireplace and kept it covered with a stock of firewood during the day.

Unfortunately, the boy became sick and was confined to his bed.

He died quickly and because no one else knew of the monkey it perished and died in its hiding place, only to return and haunt the room, scratching at the walls and wandering aimlessly at night in search of the boy."

At this I felt I must go back to the room for I had always stayed away once I had stopped using it. I wandered in and smelt the familiar musty smell that had always greeted me. The hearth looked as it had always looked with a row of neatly stacked logs on the side. One by one I pulled them away to reveal the dusted panel that sat neatly in the space behind. After some time I was able to loosen the strong grip that could only have come with age. A cloud of dust and cobwebs choked my dry throat.

As it settled I peered inside to find a small square recess and at the back in one corner lay the perfect skeleton of a small monkey. And on close inspection a small front tooth was missing from its lower jawbone.'

The Bagman's Story

By **Charles Dickens**

Adapted by Chris Mould

Taken from *The Pickwick Papers*

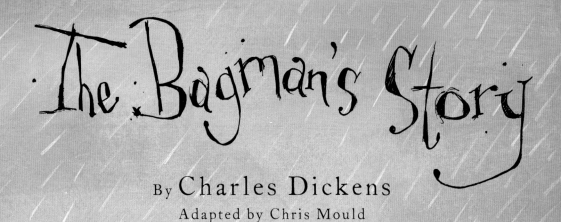

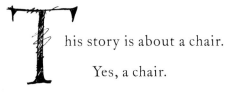

This story is about a chair.

Yes, a chair.

Not just any chair mind, but the very chair that solved old Tom Smart's problems. I don't suppose you'll believe that! Well then you'd better pull up a chair of your own (treat him kindly now) and sit back and listen.

Now Tom Smart was no great hero to be writing stories about. He was a lonely old soul with nothing but a single penny in his pocket. But everybody stumbles across a bit of good luck now and again; so I ask you, why shouldn't he?

It was no kind of night to be out but Tom Smart was fighting his way through a full force of wind and rain on his horse and cart. Before long, the mare had had enough of the weather and pulled up, of her own accord, outside a travellers' inn.

Well, it was an odd looking place, with windows and beams that jutted out here and there, but the light from a blazing fire beckoned Tom in. The bar was decorated with bottles and jars of every kind: pickles, cheeses and hams hung in wait for hungry mouths.

In less than five minutes, Tom Smart was sat by that bar and was warming his hands at the fire. But that was not all he was enjoying, for his roaming eye had fallen upon the landlady and a fine looking woman she was too, he thought.

But someone was spoiling his view. A man, a very tall man, with black whiskers and wavy hair, in a brown coat with bright basket buttons. He was seated with the woman and was making it very obvious that he thought she should be his wife.

Now Tom was fond of a tumbler of punch. He was even fonder of a tumbler or two. And as the wind blew outside until every timber in the house creaked, and as the fire roared and cracked, it seemed the very perfect idea to have a few drinks. By his fourth tumbler he was quite happy. But the more he drank, the more he thought about the woman and the tall man. Such an ugly villain, thought Tom. If the widow had any taste she might surely pick some better fellow than that.

Eventually Tom Smart decided that he had better turn in for the night and he climbed the large staircase to his room. It seemed decent enough, with a suitable bed and grand furniture. But something in particular took Tom's fancy. A strange, grim looking, high-backed chair. It was carved most intimately and the rounded knobs at the bottom of the legs were bound in red cloth like socks on as many feet. It was such a strange old thing, he could not keep his eyes off it.

I should catch my death of cold in some dusty old shop, that's what. Whereas you, Tom Smart, are a different creature. If you settled yourself in this public house you would never leave it. Not as long as there was anything to drink within its walls.'

'Well thank you for your good opinion,' said Tom.

'Therefore,' he continued, unheeding, 'you shall marry her and he shall not.'

'But how will this happen?' enquired Tom, who was finding it hard to believe that not only was he talking to a chair, but that the chair was about to solve all his money problems and provide him with a wife at the same time!

'I shall let you into a secret,' announced the old man. 'He's already married.' Then he went on to explain that the man also had six young children and that the papers that proved all this were in a particular drawer by the bed in that particular room.

Then suddenly the old man's features began to change again. He grew less and less distinct until his face had once more become the carving in the back of the chair. The waistcoat became a cushion again. The red slippers were back to small cloth bags and, as the light faded, Tom Smart fell into a deep sleep.

In the morning Tom awoke and sat up in his bed. Suddenly the events of the night before rushed upon him. He spoke to the chair. 'How are you old boy?'

Nothing. It was motionless, featureless and spoke not a word.

Perhaps he had dreamed it? But when he went to the drawer the papers were there. With an air of confidence he strolled downstairs and, taking the landlady to one side, he explained in the kindest way that circumstances were not as she had thought.

Half an hour later, he kicked the very tall man out through the front door, and a month later, he was happily married to the landlady.

And what do you suppose happened to the chair?

Well, old Tom Smart took great care of that ancient piece of furniture. You could say, he looked after that chair just as well as he looked after his wife!

The following is a true account taken from the diary of Edward Sweeney, cabin boy aboard The Armadillo, September of the year 1836, (bearings unknown).

I shall not forget that glaring look. Nor shall I forget the grip of those icy fingers upon me and the fear I held which was like no feeling I had ever had.

I need to track back a few days. I have been hard at my duties since we set sail again and not had a chance to put my pen to paper.

Somehow *The Armadillo* must have veered off its route.
We had been on course, but suddenly land appeared
up ahead of us and we could not account for it being there.

Mister Crumlin had laid some instruments out on the table and unrolled his map before the Captain, placing candlesticks at the corners to stop it springing back together again.

'See this point here,' he said, circling his forefinger on the watery mass around us, 'that's where we are now.'

'Perhaps it's too small to appear on the map,' replied the Captain.

But no, Mister Crumlin had a more detailed map of our current position. We should not have hit anything at all for another day. Something wasn't quite right, he was sure.

Captain Flynn was faced with a mystery. He wanted to make for home and fast, we all did, but we needed to stop. He walked up and down the cabin silently, rubbing his chin and contemplating his decision as Mister Crumlin stood waiting like a schoolboy.

We would stay briefly, he had announced, on account of our need for fresh fruit and in the hope of finding water. The capstan needed some minor repair work and we could take advantage of the time that the ship stood still.

I sat on the apple barrel with the sun on my face, watching the ship sway up to the island as the surf rolled on to the sand ahead of us. As we cast anchor the sun disappeared behind a cloud and what had looked, from a distance, like a picture of paradise was, on closer inspection, a cold and unnerving place. A tattered old skull and cross-boned flag was draped from a tree in a display of warning. We had often seen these in the past. They were not uncommon.

There was no sign of life and certainly no other vessel to speak of but Captain Flynn was hesitant.

A rowing boat was sent in first to check out the island.

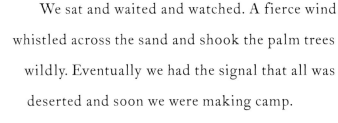

We sat and waited and watched. A fierce wind whistled across the sand and shook the palm trees wildly. Eventually we had the signal that all was deserted and soon we were making camp.

It felt good to stand on solid ground again and we split into small groups to settle in. I was instructed to collect driftwood. An inlet gave way to several cave-like openings in the rocks and so off I went, half of me excited and the other half frightened to death that I might meet some marooned scoundrel who would cut me to pieces. I laughed at myself and carried on; there was a job to do.

I had gone quite a distance when up ahead I saw a tree. It was old and gnarled and surely dead. It looked a bit like a bony, upturned hand. The wood was dry and would burn easily. It seemed hollow and I was able to pull away the outside like a shell. As I did so, I fell backward and tumbled down a small hummock into a pile of rocks. A small opening stared at me and beckoned me in. One chamber led into another and then another. I had no real taste for this adventure but something pulled me onward.

Suddenly, I was staring straight at something that took my breath away. A crumbling, dusty skeleton lay heaped in a corner. A nest of cobwebs held every inch of his frame together. He was dressed in nothing but a bandanna and a buckled belt about his waist. A rusted hook made the hand on the end of his left arm and he clung tightly on to the small barrel that was in his arms. It held a thousand twinkling golden pieces. I was so shocked that I didn't move for quite some time.

At first I hesitated, but then I could not resist. I held the glistening gold in my hands. I let it pour through my fingers. And then I ran – as fast as I had ever done – back to our camp to tell the others.

Soon we were all stood there. We looked on in amazement at the sight before us. Captain Flynn had no interest in the gold. 'We must leave it,' he said, 'and be away from this place, for it only promises trouble.' And that was all he said on the matter. Treasure hunting was a desperate business and not for the likes of us merchant sailors.

We turned around and returned to camp but I must confess that earlier, I had slipped three doubloons into my pocket and promised myself I would put them back when I brought the others. I never did, and before long I was to regret it.

The Captain had been reluctant to stay the night but our distractions had wasted time and it was growing dark. We were used to the sound of parrots and all kinds of tree-dwelling animals but here there was nothing. The night grew icy cold and we huddled into the fire. Eventually we settled and it must have been well into the early hours before we were sleeping.

In the morning there was fevered excitement. We had all dreamed the same dream. A hundred pirates with missing limbs and hooked hands lurched at us in our slumber. They growled and screamed, clutching and gasping and tearing at us like animals. They tore at our throats and beat us with cudgels and muskets. Some of us had cried out in the night and awoken the others. The Captain refused to join our talk of pirates and had no fascination for these dreams.

I knew I should try and return the coins for I now feared they would bring us harm. Yet to do so would prove difficult for I would have to break from my duties and I would be gone for too long. I could not let the Captain know I had taken them. He thought much of me. I had worked hard to gain his respect and I did not want to disappoint him. Alas, I was unable to carry out my task and I held on to my prize nervously as we boarded *The Armadillo* once again.

It felt good to be back. Our stock of fruit was healthy and we had found fresh water. Repairs had been made to the ship too and we were in better shape now than when we had stopped. The anchor was lifted and we were steered back on course.

The Captain was greatly relieved at our departure and a confidence had returned to the crew that I felt had been missing on the island. By early evening we were well on course, heading into the sun. Mister Crumlin kept his assurance that we were on target and I went about my duties.

Our fantasies of murderous pirates had passed and our thoughts turned to the way home. I sat on the apple barrel and watched the night roll in and soon we were in darkness again. I turned to my work below deck where I helped Cook with the meal.

Soon we were at the table. I had always enjoyed the company of the crew. I loved to listen to their old sea stories as they drank into the night and they had always made me welcome. Sometimes they would rib me and poke fun but I did not mind. I suppose I enjoyed it. It made me feel a part of the group.

By the time we had finished our chores it was late so I took to the sleeping quarters while the men carried on drinking. I lay alone in my hammock and fell asleep listening to their laughing and drunken singing as I had always done.

I awoke with a start in the black of night and sat up in my hammock. I must have screamed for the quartermaster burst in. 'Yer all right Sweeney?' he asked.

'Just dreaming,' I said. 'Thank you.'

He closed the door. But as he did so, right there, in the corner where it had leaned open, stood the ghostly figure of the deadliest of pirates. He was dripping wet. A pool of saltwater circled his feet. Dressed in black he bore a rusted cutlass strapped at his waist. A deathly white skeletal frame dangled out of his long musty coat and his face grinned and glowed through the darkness. I was so struck with horror I could not raise a noise of any kind.

Suddenly without warning, he raced at me, clutching at my throat with bony hands. I felt his salty breath upon my face. His reddened eyes pierced through mine. Then he ripped at my pocket until the three coins fell to the deck. He scraped at the floorboards and held them in his fingers. Then, as quickly as he had arrived, he turned and fled, floating downwards through the floor of the ship as if to return to some ancient dead man's locker below the sea.

I rubbed my eyes and lit my candle for a moment. The light would help to steady my nerves. Surely I was still dreaming. I walked over to the corner where he had stood to make sure that nothing was there.

The floor was wet.

I ran my hand down to my pocket. It was torn and the three coins had gone.

The Phantom Coach

By Amelia B. Edwards

Adapted by Chris Mould

*I*t was a cold December evening on a wide, bleak moor in the north of England and I was lost. The first flakes of a snowstorm fluttered down upon the heather.

I stared nervously into the gathering darkness. I could do nothing while the whiteness thickened and the cold bit harder. I remembered stories of travellers who walked on through falling snow until at last, worn out, they lay down and died.

Then, a wavering speck of light came out of the dark, growing nearer and nearer. To my joy, I soon came face to face with a man carrying a lantern. 'Thank goodness,' I cried out.

'What for?' he growled. (I have to say, he was not as pleased to see me as I was to see him.)

'Where is the nearest village?' I questioned. 'And where do you live?'

'Nearest village is Wyke, nigh on twelve miles, but I live out that way,' he answered, with a vague jerk of his lantern.

'Then I'm coming with you,' I announced.

'It ain't no use,' he said, 'the master won't let you in.'

'We'll see about that,' I replied briskly. 'You lead the way and I'll suggest that he should give me food and shelter for the night.'

'You can try!' he muttered, and shaking his head, he hobbled gnome-like through the falling snow.

Soon we reached the house. The door was studded with iron nails like a prison entrance. A large dog ran up, barking furiously. 'Down boy,' growled my companion, as he fumbled in his pocket for a key.

Once inside I found myself in a great raftered hall and was sent through a low door to another room. A white-haired old man rose from a table covered with books and papers. 'Who are you?' he began. 'How did you come here and what do you want?'

'My name is James Murray, sir, and I only seek rest and a meal to help me along my way. I was lost in the thickening snow and had no choice but to seek help.'

He pulled aside a heavy black curtain and peered out. 'You can stay, if you choose, till morning unless the snow stops earlier. Jacob, serve the supper.' With this he waved me to a seat and we ate in complete silence. I drew back my chair to the fireplace and rested a while.

Later, my host rose from his chair and stood at the window to announce that the snow had stopped. 'The night mail coach from the north changes horses at Dwolding. It will be due at the crossroads in just over an hour. If Jacob were to take you across the moor he could put you on to the old coach route. You could find your way from there,' he suggested.

Within minutes Jacob was locking the door and we were out on the moor again. It was bitterly cold. The snow crunched beneath our feet. I strode on at the heels of my guide until suddenly he came to a halt. 'There's yer road,' he said, pointing. 'Mind where the parapet's broken further down. It's never been mended since the accident.'

'What accident?' I enquired.

'It was the night mail. Pitched right over into the valley below –

a good fifty feet or more. Four were found dead and t'other two died next morning.'

'When was this?'

'Just nine year,' he said. And at this warning Jacob turned and left, trudging back the way he had come. I watched the light from his lantern disappear and then I was alone again. I walked on.

Shortly afterwards I was relieved to see another light drawing nearer. It was the light from two carriage lamps. They grew brighter and I could see the shape of the carriage. It came fast but without any noise. The snow was a foot deep under the wheels.

I jumped forward, waving my hat and shouting. At first I thought I had gone unnoticed but the coach pulled up sharply ahead of me. Neither the driver nor the outside passenger acknowledged me. I looked inside at the three travellers and slipped into the vacant corner.

If it were possible, it seemed colder inside than it was out. A damp and disagreeable smell filled the air. I looked at my fellow passengers. All three were men and remained silent. Each was leaning back in his corner of the vehicle. 'How terribly cold it is tonight,' I said.

My opposite neighbour lifted his head. He stared at me through the darkness but made no reply. I shivered from head to foot but the smell inside became so sickly that I asked the man to my left if he would object to my opening the window. He neither spoke nor stirred and so, losing my patience, I let the sash down abruptly.

83

The strap broke in my hand. I looked around the rest of the coach. The leather fittings were crusted with mould. The floor was breaking away at my feet. The whole thing was foul with damp. I turned to the third passenger. 'This coach is in terrible condition,' I moaned.

Slowly he moved his head and stared into my face without uttering a word. I shall never forget that look as long as I live. My sight had grown used to the dark and I could suddenly see quite distinctly. His eyes glared a fiery glow inside a gruesome skeletal face. A dreadful horror came upon me. I turned to my travelling companions. They all stared at me with the same ghostly shine in their eyes. None of them were living men. A pale phosphorescent light played upon their deathly faces. Their hair was dank and muddied from the grave. Their clothes were earth-stained and shredded in pieces. Only their eyes, their terrible eyes were living, and they were all turned on me.

A shriek of terror burst from my lips as I flung myself against the door to open it. In that moment I saw the broken parapet, the plunging horses and the valley below. The coach reeled like a ship at sea, turning over and over; a mighty crash followed, a sense of crushing pain and then darkness...

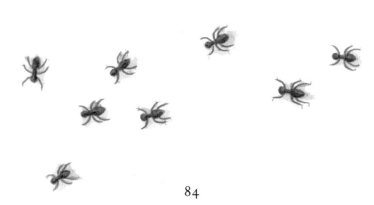

It seemed as if years had gone by when I awoke one morning from a deep sleep and found my wife at my side. Apparently I had fallen over the edge and was only saved from death by a snowdrift. I was discovered at daybreak by two shepherds and found in a terrible state with a broken arm and fractured skull.

The place of my accident, need I say it, was exactly the point where the north mail had gone over the edge nine years before. I never told my wife the whole story and others will form what conclusions they choose, but I know that all those years ago on that night, I was the fourth passenger inside the phantom coach.

The very Last Train

By Chris Mould

What a ghastly noise it was, screaming and hollering, piercing the night air. That and the ghostly echoes of clickety-clack, clickety-clack, and the reeling and squeaking of the track.

And oh, what a terrifying sight to see, as the carriages hurtled out of the tunnel like a pack of crazy animals nose to tail, with every horrid form of spectre and spirit looming from its windows, clinging on for dear death. And all along being pulled by the monstrous, blackened shape of the engine that raced like a bullet into darkness.

That was how his grandmother had described it anyway, all those years ago. 'Straight from the mouth of hell,' she said, for that was what they called the tunnel from whence it came: as black as night and plastered in soot, it was a low bridge with loose bricks that jutted out

and down, 'like devils teeth,' she said. A crooked oak tree pointed
its fingers towards the black hole in warning.

But Granville Grunt didn't believe in such nonsense.
His imagination didn't stretch so far. Sure, it was fine to tell tales around
the fire but it held no more weight than that, he would say. He didn't have
time for fantasy. There was too much work to be done and nothing else
to think about except himself and all the troubles that buzzed around
his head like little flies. And then there was all the moaning and
grumbling that went with it that made everything take twice as long
and so there really wasn't time. But somehow, on this particular night
he had ended up on that particular platform and was staring right into
that particular tunnel...

Grunt had been late at the office again and had missed his usual
train. Before he knew it the clock was close to twelve and he would have
to catch the twilight service which boarded on the other side of town.
He would have to walk a good deal further but at least he would have
something to complain about. So on he went. He was getting too old for
all this, he had thought to himself.

Well that was true. Old and miserable he was. From the holes in
his shoes to the tip of his moth-eaten hat, he was every inch the grumpy
old fossil.

And on he went, lolloping down the road in the dark, bandy legged
and stringy, gasping and wheezing and falling apart at the seams with
his clapped-out umbrella held high up over his head. The rain poured

through the holes and drenched his
aching bones. He rushed
and gasped and looked at
his watch and then rushed a bit
more. He stopped to catch his
breath in a doorway.

Suddenly he was at the station.
As he stood there on the
platform he remembered his
grandmother and the story she
had told him and, all at once,
he felt that little bit colder.

The old tree was still there
and the tunnel looked almost
overgrown with great stretches
of ivy. The whole place looked
like it hadn't been used in years.
He didn't really want to be
standing right there at
midnight. Not that he
was scared, of course.

Oh no, that knocking of his knees was down to the cold weather, he knew that. Of course he did, he knew everything.

When it reached twelve o'clock he realised he might have missed his train but then he heard the reassuring thumpety-thump of wheels pounding the tracks. And his heart sank. Thud. He almost heard it hit the floor.

Out of the darkness roared the ghostly black engine of the phantom train. Two huge headlamps threw a glow of light across the platform. A pair of screaming skeletons, braced together, formed a cowcatcher at the front end. Steam and sparks billowed out from the crooked chimney. An endless line of carriages rushed on behind, bounding and leaping with a sea of staring faces, grinning teeth and clutching hands reaching out.

Now there was one thing that his grandmother hadn't told him. Maybe she knew and maybe she didn't. But if you did happen to see that train then it meant that you were already dead yourself. And when the last carriage was about to pass you by, some cold stranger's skeleton arms would reach out and grab you. They'd pull you on board and drag your soul all the way down to the very pits of the earth.

Do you know what? That's exactly what happened to Granville Grunt.

And the next morning his sad, pathetic figure was found curled up in a doorway across town, halfway between the two stations.

Well, my friend,
I'm afraid I can't take you
any further.
The sun is rising and

I'm not too keen on daylight.
I hope you enjoyed your journey.
Maybe we'll meet again some night
on another darkened road...